9,99,-

110520-15

Koen Van Biesen has illustrated over twenty children's books, including *Roger Is Reading a Book* (Eerdmans). He lives in Belgium and teaches at the Academy of Fine Arts in Mortsel. Visit his website at www.koenvanbiesen.com.

For Matteo

This book was published with the support of the Flemish Literature Fund. (www.flemishliterature.be).

The illustrations were created using mixed media. The display and text type was set in Bureau Grotesque.

First published in the United States in 2017 by
Eerdmans Books for Young Readers,
an imprint of Wm. B. Eerdmans Publishing Co.
2140 Oak Industrial Dr. NE, Grand Rapids, Michigan 49505
www.eerdmans.com/youngreaders

Originally published in Belgium in 2015 under the title
Buurman Vangt Een Vis by Uitgeverij De Eenhoorn bvba
Vlasstraat 17, B-8710 Wielsbeke, Belgium
Text and illustrations © Koen Van Biesen
© 2015 Uitgeverij De Eenhoorn bvba
English language translation © 2017 Laura Watkinson

23 22 21 20 19 18 17   9 8 7 6 5 4 3 2 1

ISBN 978-0-8028-5491-9

A catalog record of this book is available from the Library of Congress.

ROGER
IS GOING FISHING

Koen Van Biesen

Translated by **Laura Watkinson**

Eerdmans Books for Young Readers

BUMBLE-DE-BUMP! BUMBLE-DE-BUMP!

Roger riding, Bob in the basket, Emily in back.

STEP STEP STEP STEP ST

ROGER! ROGER!

I've got a bite!

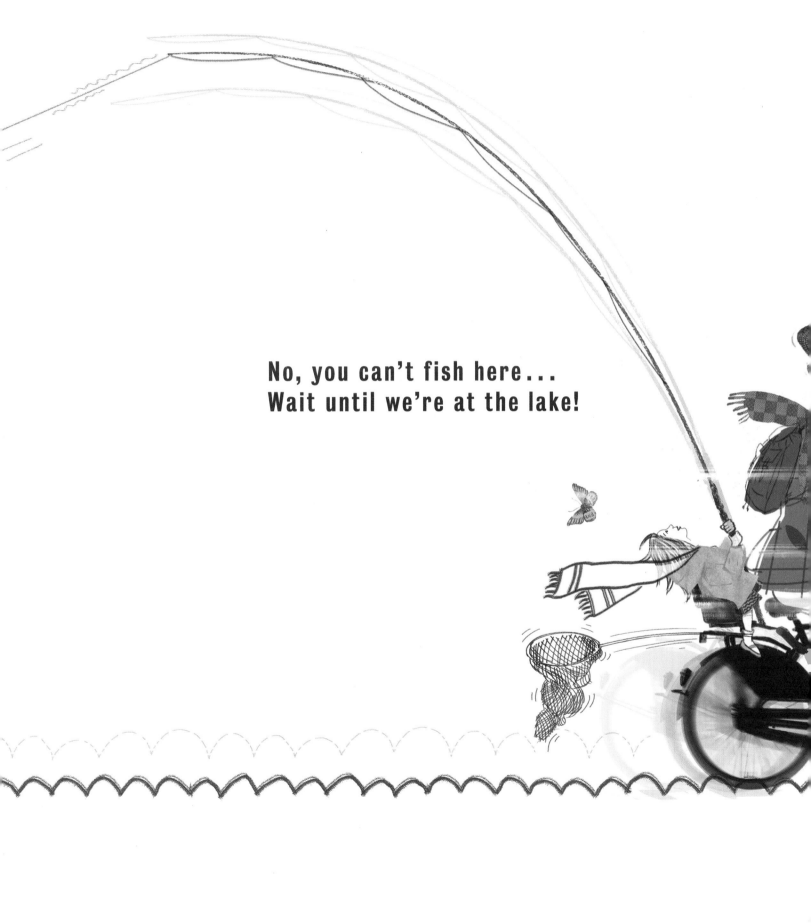

No, you can't fish here...
Wait until we're at the lake!

STOP! STOP!

BUMBLE-DE-BUMP! BUMBLE-DE-BUMP!

Roger riding, Bob in the basket, Emily in back.

SHOP SHOP SHOP SHOP SH

ROGER! ROGER!

I've got a bite...

No, you can't fish here...
Wait until we're at the lake!

BUMBLE-DE-BUMP! BUMBLE-DE-BUMP!

Roger riding, Bob in the basket, Emily in back.

HIP HOP
HIP HOP
H

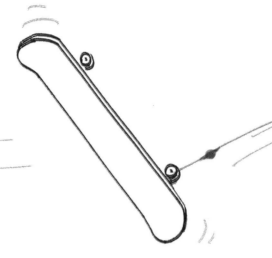

ROGER! ROGER!

I've got a bite....

No, you can't fish here...
Wait until we're at the lake!

Stop! Stop! Stop! Stop! Stop! Stop!

BUMBLE-DE-BUMP! BUMBLE-DE-BUMP!

Roger riding, Bob in the basket,

Emily in back.

LA LA LA

DUM DUM DUM

R...R...R...ROOOOOOOOOOO

OOOOOOOOOOGER!

Hang on, Emily,
let me guess:
you've got a bite?

HEY HEY HEY
three sheep eating hay

BAA **BAA** BAA

BAA BAA BAA

HEY HEY HEY MOo

three sheep and
one cow too

MOo MOO

KRRR...KRRR...   No one sees or hears us as we pass,

only the crickets in the grass ...   No one?

GLUG...GLUG...GLUG

Emily, hey, I got my wish!
Look, I caught
a great big ...

caramba

9,99,-